Five reasons we think you'll love Winnie and Wilbur AT THE SEASIDE

When she's not wearing stripy tights, Winnie has a stripy swimsuit!

There is so much to spot in every picture.

Winnie shares the beach with lots of funny characters.

You're bound to have a whale of a time!

You can take the... ...challenge: can you spot someone rea... ...Wilbur picture book?

Freya

Anushka

Maggie

Bailey

Johannes

Molly

Ashley

Amber

Jun-Yeong

Pablo

Matilda

Marwin

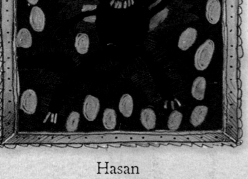

Hasan

Rebecca

Thank you to all these schools for
helping with the endpapers:

St Barnabas Primary School, Oxford; St Ebbe's Primary
School, Oxford; Marcham Primary School, Abingdon; St
Michael's C.E. Aided Primary School, Oxford; St Bede's
RC Primary School, Jarrow; The Western Academy,
Beijing, China; John King School, Pinxton; Neston
Primary School, Neston; Star of the Sea RC Primary
School, Whitley Bay; José Jorge Letria Primary School,
Cascais, Portugal; Dunmore Primary School, Abingdon;
Özel Bahçeşehir İlköğretim Okulu, Istanbul, Turkey; the
International School of Amsterdam, the Netherlands;
Princethorpe Infant School, Birmingham.

For Margaret Coram,
Winnie's greatest fan—V.T.

To Oliver James Johnson—
K.P

OXFORD
UNIVERSITY PRESS

Great Clarendon Street, Oxford OX2 6DP

Oxford University Press is a department of the University
of Oxford. It furthers the University's objective of
excellence in research, scholarship, And education by
publishing worldwide. Oxford is a registered trade mark
of Oxford University Press in the UK and in certain other countries

Database right Oxford University Press (maker)

First published as *Winnie at the Seaside* in 2005
This edition first published in 2016

British Library Cataloguing in Publication Data available

ISBN: 978-0-19-274822-5 (paperback)
ISBN: 978-0-19-274912-3 (paperback and CD)

10 9 8 7 6 5 4 3 2 1

Printed in China

Paper used in the production of this book is a natural, recyclable product made
from wood grown in sustainable forests. The manufacturing process conforms
to the environmental regulations of the country of origin

www.winnieandwilbur.com

VALERIE THOMAS AND KORKY PAUL

Winnie AND Wilbur
AT THE SEASIDE

OXFORD
UNIVERSITY PRESS

It was a very hot summer.
Winnie the Witch felt hot and tired.
Wilbur, her cat, felt hot and tired, too.
'I want a swim, Wilbur,' Winnie said.
'Let's go to the seaside.'

Winnie found her beach towel, her
beach bag and her beach umbrella.

She jumped onto her broomstick,
Wilbur jumped onto her shoulder,
and they were off.

They flew over hot towns,
hot roads, hot cars,
and then they came to the sea.

There were lots of people on the beach,
but Winnie found a place for her towel.

She put up her beach umbrella
and got ready for her swim.

'Look after my bag and my broomstick, Wilbur,' Winnie said.
She ran into the water.

It was lovely in the sea.
Winnie splashed through the water,
and skipped over the little waves.
She was having a lovely time.

Wilbur sat and watched her.
He couldn't swim. He didn't like water.
He hated getting wet.

Winnie dived into the water. It was such fun!

But the water started to creep up the sand,
up to Winnie's towel.

Wilbur jumped onto
Winnie's beach umbrella.
'Meeow,' he cried.

Then the sea picked Winnie up, turned her over
three times, and dumped her on the sand.

The water washed over Winnie's towel,
and came half way up Winnie's beach bag.

'Meeeooooww,' cried Wilbur.
He didn't want to get wet.

'Oh dear,' said Winnie. She shook
some seaweed out of her hair.

'Don't worry, Wilbur.
We'll just move further up the beach.'

She picked up her beach bag and her towel.
'My broomstick!' cried Winnie. 'Where's my broomstick?'

She looked everywhere.

No broomstick.

Then she looked out to sea.
There was her broomstick, floating away.

'Stop!' Winnie shouted.
But her broomstick didn't stop.

'How will we get home, Wilbur?' cried Winnie.
Then she had an idea.
She grabbed her beach bag, took out her
magic wand, waved it five times, and shouted,

'Abracadabra!'

The broomstick stopped.

Then it started to come back.

But a surfer was in the way.

Whoosh

went the broomstick,
high up in the air,
and it landed on a whale.

The whale didn't want a broomstick on its back.

Whoosh

went the broomstick, high up in the air,
in a great spout of water.

Splash!

Winnie's broomstick had come back.
Winnie was pleased.

The other people on the beach
were not pleased at all.

They were very WET.

Wilbur was not pleased either.

He was very wet, very sandy,
and rather squashed.

'Oh dear,' Winnie said. 'We'd better go home, Wilbur.'
She packed everything up.

Then Winnie and Wilbur zoomed up into the sky.

They were soon home again.
It was still hot in Winnie's garden.
Winnie still felt hot and tired.

Then she had a wonderful idea.

She took her magic wand out of her beach bag,
shut her eyes, turned around three times,
and shouted,

'Abracadabra!'

There in her garden was
a beautiful swimming pool.

Winnie dived in.

She swam up and down, and
then she floated on her back.

'This is lovely, Wilbur,' she said.
'It's much nicer than the seaside.'

Anything is nicer than the seaside,
thought Wilbur.

Bethany

Katia

Eun-Jae

Kathleen

Ji-Eun

Jenny

Sara

Fraser

Ka Keung

Selin

Selin

Olivia

Siyabend

Kieran

A note for grown-ups

Oxford Owl is a FREE and easy-to-use website packed with support and advice about everything to do with reading.

Informative videos

Hints, tips and fun activities

Top tips from top writers for reading with your child

Help with choosing picture books

For this expert advice and much, much more about how children learn to read and how to keep them reading ...

LOOK
for Oxford Owl
www.oxfordowl.co.uk